Felicia's
FAVORITE
Story

BY LESLÉA NEWMAN
ILLUSTRATED BY ADRIANA ROMO

Two Lives Publishing

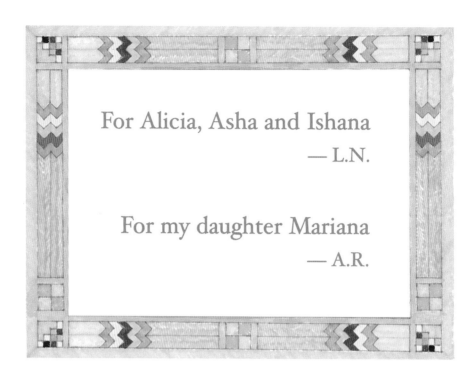

For Alicia, Asha and Ishana
— L.N.

For my daughter Mariana
— A.R.

Published by
Two Lives Publishing
508 North Swarthmore Avenue
Ridley Park, PA 19078

Visit our website: www.TwoLives.com

ISBN: 0-9674468-5-6

LCCN: 2002109054

1 2 3 4 5 6 7 8 9 10

Printed in China

Felicia put the last piece of her Animals Around the World puzzle in place just as the clock above the kitchen table chimed eight times. Mama Nessa looked up from the pot she was scrubbing.

"It's eight o'clock, Felicia," she said. "You know what that means."

"Bedtime." Felicia made a face.

"I have an idea." Mama Linda finished wiping off the stove and sat down at the table. "If you put on your pajamas and brush your teeth quick as a bunny, I'll come upstairs and read you a story."

"I want Mama Nessa to come, too," Felicia said.

"I'll come up right after I finish these dishes," Mama Nessa said, as she rinsed out a cup.

Felicia ran upstairs and put on her favorite pajamas, the yellow ones with the soft, puffy sleeves. Then she brushed her teeth, hopped into bed and yelled, "I'm ready!"

"Ready or not, here I come," Mama Linda called as she climbed the steps.

"Which book would you like to hear?" asked Mama Linda, kneeling down in front of Felicia's bookcase.

"I don't want to hear a book," Felicia said. "I want to hear a story."

"Which story would you like me to tell?" Mama Linda asked.

"My very favorite story," Felicia said.

"Your very favorite story..." Mama Linda repeated, as though she were trying to remember. "Which story is that?"

"You know," Felicia cried. "The story of how I was adopted."

"Oh, that story." Mama Linda smiled as she sat down on Felicia's bed which was soft as a cloud and began.

"Once upon a time there was a woman named Linda..."

"That's you," said Felicia.

"...and a woman named Vanessa."

"That's Mama Nessa," said Felicia.

"That's right," said Mama Linda. "And they lived in a little house with curtains the color of sunshine in the window and a roof the color of..."

"The moon!" Felicia said.

"Vanessa and Linda were very happy together," continued Mama Linda. "They loved each other very much. One day Vanessa said to Linda, 'We have so much love between us, let's find someone else who can share our love and be part of our family.' Linda thought that was a wonderful idea."

Mama Linda looked at Felicia, "So, who do you think became part of our family?"

"A giraffe?" asked Felicia.

"No," said Mama Linda. "A giraffe was too tall to come into the house and read stories with us."

"How about a mouse?" asked Felicia.

"No," said Mama Linda. "A mouse was too small to sit at the kitchen table and eat breakfast with us."

Felicia thought for a minute. "I know," she said. "A baby became part of your family."

"That's right," said Mama Linda. "A baby became part of our family. Now, where do you think our baby came from?"

"Puerto Rico?" asked Felicia.

"No," said Mama Linda. "I was born in Puerto Rico, but that isn't where our baby was born."

"How about New York?" asked Felicia.

"No," said Mama Linda. "Mama Nessa was born in New York, but our baby wasn't born there either."

Felicia thought for a minute. "I know," she said. "Your baby was born in Guatemala."

"That's right," said Mama Linda. "Our baby was born in a beautiful country called Guatemala. Sometimes, Felicia," Mama Linda said, "when a woman has a baby, she isn't able to take care of the child. So she does the most loving thing she can do: she allows the child to be adopted by parents who can take care of a baby and who want a child to love. Such a woman lived in Guatemala, so that's where Mama Nessa and I went. Now, how do you think we got there?"

"Did you drive the car?" asked Felicia.

"No," said Mama Linda. "We almost drove the car, but that would have taken a very long time."

"And you were in a great big hurry," said Felicia.

Mama Linda laughed. "Yes, we were."

"Did you take a boat?" asked Felicia.

"No," said Mama Linda. "We almost took a boat, but the captain said that would take a long time, too."

Felicia thought for a minute. "I know," she said. "You flew in an airplane."

"That's right," said Mama Linda. "Mama Nessa and I flew to Guatemala in a big silver airplane. And when we got there, a baby girl with big brown eyes and shiny black hair was waiting for us."

"And the baby girl was me!" Felicia cried.

"That's right," said Mama Linda. "But you were much smaller than you are now."

"Was I small as a button?" asked Felicia, pointing to a yellow button on her pajama top.

"No," said Mama Linda. "You were bigger than that."

"Was I small as a cookie?" asked Felicia, holding her fingers in a circle the size of the oatmeal cookies she and Mama Nessa had baked that afternoon.

"No," said Mama Linda. "You were bigger than that."

Felicia thought for a minute. "I know," she said. "I was small as Rosa." Felicia held her teddy bear up in the air.

"That's right," said Mama Linda. "You were small as Rosa. And as soon as Mama Nessa and I saw you, we knew we loved you and wanted you to be part of our family."

"And as soon as I saw you and Mama Nessa," Felicia said, "I cried."

"That's right," said Mama Linda.

"But only for a minute," Felicia reminded her.

"Yes," said Mama Linda. "Only for a minute. You stopped crying as soon as Mama Nessa and I picked you up and held you in our arms. After that, you hardly cried at all, even on the big silver airplane we flew home in, and it was a very long ride."

"That's right," said Mama Nessa, as she stepped into Felicia's room. "Everyone on the big silver airplane admired you and said what a good baby you were. And so we named you Felicia, a Spanish name which means..."

"Funny," said Felicia, making a silly face.

"No, no, no," said Mama Nessa with a laugh. "Felicia is a Spanish name which means..."

"Sad," said Felicia, looking as though she were about to cry.

"No, no, no," said Mama Linda, wiping a make-believe tear off Felicia's cheek. "Felicia is a Spanish name which means..."

"Scary," said Felicia, making a terrible face and speaking in a deep growling voice.

"No, no, no," said Mama Nessa and Mama Linda, jumping back in fright. "Felicia," they said together, "is a Spanish name which means..."

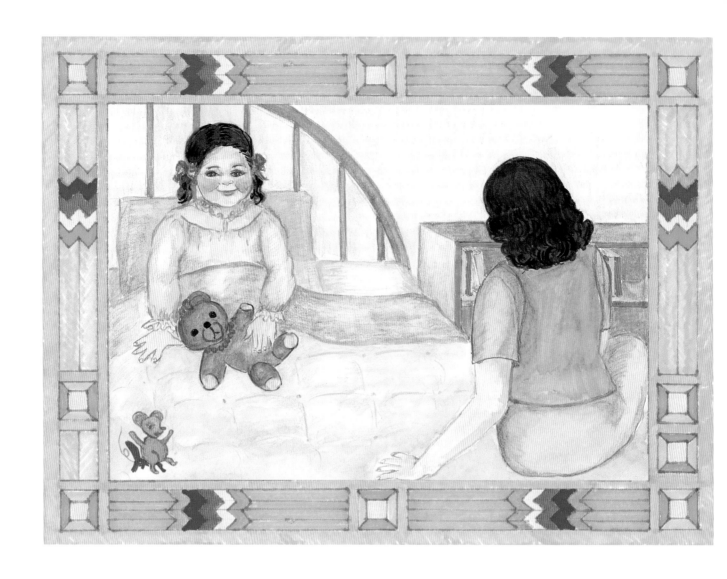

"Happy," said Felicia, with a great big smile.

"That's right," said Mama Nessa. "We named you Felicia because you were such a happy baby and because having you in our family makes Mama Linda and me very, very happy."

And Felicia fell happily asleep.

Mary Vazquez

Lesléa Newman has published many award-winning books for children including *Heather Has Two Mommies, Too Far Away to Touch, Runaway Dreidel!, Matzo Ball Moon, Dogs, Dogs, Dogs!* and *Cats, Cats, Cats!* She has received a Highlights for Children fiction-writing award and a Parents' Choice Silver Medal. Ms. Newman lives in Northampton, Massachusetts. Visit *www.lesleakids.com* to learn more about her books for children.

ABOUT THE ILLUSTRATOR

Born in Chile, in 1929, Adriana Romo has always made art for her family: paintings, illustrations, puppets and marionettes, and more recently, a memoir of her childhood. She and her husband arrived in the United States in 1966, have three children and one grandson, and currently live in New York City. Adriana received her degree in fine arts from the University of Connecticut in 1983.

Mariana Romo-Carmona